Little Shaq

**Books by Shaquille O'Neal and
illustrated by Theodore Taylor III**

Little Shaq
Little Shaq Takes a Chance
Little Shaq: Star of the Week

Little Shaq

SHAQUILLE O'NEAL

illustrated by
Theodore Taylor III

BLOOMSBURY
NEW YORK LONDON OXFORD NEW DELHI SYDNEY

To my loving parents and my wonderful children
—Shaquille

To my wife, Sarah, and my son, Theo
—Theodore

Text copyright © 2015 by Shaquille O'Neal
Illustrations copyright © 2015 by Theodore Taylor III
All rights reserved. No part of this book may be reproduced or transmitted in any form
or by any means, electronic or mechanical, including photocopying, recording, or by any
information storage and retrieval system, without permission in writing from the publisher.

First published in the United States of America in October 2015
by Bloomsbury Children's Books
Paperback edition published in October 2016
www.bloomsbury.com

Bloomsbury is a registered trademark of Bloomsbury Publishing Plc

Shaquille O'Neal™; Rights of Publicity and Persona Rights: ABG-Shaq, LLC. shaq.com

For information about permission to reproduce selections from this book, write to
Permissions, Bloomsbury Children's Books, 1385 Broadway, New York, New York 10018
Bloomsbury books may be purchased for business or promotional use. For information on bulk
purchases please contact Macmillan Corporate and Premium Sales Department at
specialmarkets@macmillan.com

Library of Congress Cataloging-in-Publication Data
O'Neal, Shaquille.
Little Shaq / by Shaquille O'Neal ; illustrated by Theodore Taylor III.
pages   cm
Summary: Seven-year-old Shaquille O'Neal, a talented basketball and video game player,
learns to share the spotlight with his cousin Barry when the youngsters
work together to earn money by watering plants.
ISBN 978-1-61963-721-4 (hardcover)
ISBN 978-1-61963-813-6 (e-book) • ISBN 978-1-61963-867-9 (e-PDF)
1. O'Neal, Shaquille—Childhood and youth—Fiction. [1. O'Neal, Shaquille—Childhood and youth—
Fiction. 2. Cousins—Fiction. 3. Moneymaking projects—Fiction. 4. Teamwork (Sports)—Fiction.
5. Gardening—Fiction. 6. African Americans—Fiction.] I. Taylor, Theodore, III, illustrator. II. Title.
PZ7.O549Li 2015   [Fic]—dc23   2014038765

ISBN 978-1-61963-722-1 (paperback)

Art created digitally
Typeset in Chaparral, Housearama Kingpin, and Shag Expert Lounge • Book design by John Candell
Printed in China by C&C Offset Printing Co., Ltd., Shenzhen, Guangdong
1 3 5 7 9 10 8 6 4 2

All papers used by Bloomsbury Publishing, Inc., are natural, recyclable products
made from wood grown in well-managed forests. The manufacturing processes
conform to the environmental regulations of the country of origin.

Table of Contents

Chapter 1
SLAM DUNK

Little Shaq dribbled the basketball, bouncing it up and down.

He moved his feet from side to side. His sneakers squeaked against the court.

"Come on, Little Shaq. Pass me the ball!" his cousin Barry shouted. Barry's voice sounded far away.

The game clock
was down to five
seconds. If Little
Shaq scored this
basket, his team would win the
game!

"I'm open. I'm
open!" Barry yelled.
Little Shaq took
a deep breath. The
clock ticked down.
Three . . . two . . .

Little Shaq's friend Walter
Skipple raised his arms to block
the ball, but he wasn't fast enough.
With one quick leap, Little Shaq shot
the ball into the air. It flew off his
fingertips toward the basket.

SWISH!

The ball slid through the net just as
the buzzer sounded.

BEEEEEP!

"Nothin' but net!" Little Shaq

cheered. "We won!"

"Great shot, Little Shaq," said

Walter. "Next time, you're on my

team!"

Little Shaq looked around the gym to say "good game" to Barry, but he couldn't find him anywhere.

"Nice effort, everyone," Coach Mackins said. "See you all here tomorrow."

Little Shaq ran to get his backpack from the bench.

His next-door neighbor Rosa Lindy was sitting in the bleachers.

"Did you see where Barry went?" he asked her.

Rosa looked up from her book of puzzles. She shook her head no.

Little Shaq sighed.

Whenever Barry left the game by himself, he was mad about something.

Outside, Barry kicked at the dirt along the edge of the rec center's dried-up garden.

He was waiting for Nana Ruth to pick them all up.

"There you are, Barry!" Little Shaq called.

Barry didn't answer and turned
his head away.

Little Shaq felt his tummy sink.

Barry wasn't only mad, he was mad at Little Shaq.

On the drive home Rosa chatted with Nana Ruth, but Barry just stared out the window.

Little Shaq knew he had to do something.

He tried making
funny faces. He
tried making silly
noises. He tried
everything!

    Nothing would make

Barry talk.

"Hey, Barry,"
Little Shaq
said finally. "Wanna
play *Ultimate Pro Jams*
when we get to my house?"

Ultimate Pro Jams was Little Shaq's and Barry's favorite basketball video game.

"You can be Player One," he added, hoping this would cheer Barry up.

"Really?" Barry asked, turning around.

Player One got to name the team *and* pick the jerseys. Being Player One was the best.

"Sure!" said Little Shaq.

Barry thought for a moment

while Nana Ruth parked outside Little Shaq's house. "Well, okay," he replied.

Little Shaq and Barry ran inside and changed their clothes before heading to the family room.

Rosa had already snuggled onto the sofa with her book.

"Let's name our team the O'Neal Tigers," said Little Shaq.

Little Shaq and Barry had the same last name, so the first part was easy, but they didn't always agree on the mascot. Little Shaq liked cats, and Barry liked birds.

"But Barry is Player One, so he gets to pick the name," said Rosa.

"Besides, you were the Tigers two games ago."

Rosa was the smartest girl in Little Shaq's class. She had a great memory.

Sometimes Little Shaq just wished that she didn't remember *everything*.

"Tigers are the coolest, Rosa," Little Shaq replied. "They are the kings of the jungle!"

"That's lions!" Barry laughed.

Barry typed "O'Neal Falcons" onto the screen and pressed Play.

Their team started out with the ball.

Barry's player dribbled it down the court, but the defense came on strong.

"Watch out!" Little Shaq shouted as a player reached in and stole the ball, taking it back the other way.

"You gotta protect the ball, Barry," he said.

"I know," Barry replied.

"Here, watch me," Little Shaq said as his player grabbed the ball from Barry's after a rebound.

Little Shaq turned his player's back to the defense and moved him down the court.

"I did that before," Barry said. "And I can do lots of things that *you* can't."

"Oh yeah?" said Little Shaq. "Well, I bet you can't do *this*."

Little Shaq gripped his controller tight and hit two buttons at once.

His player soared across the court,

high into the air, and reached for the net.

With another push of a button, Little Shaq spun his player around and jammed the ball through the basket.

"Slam dunk!" Little Shaq shouted.

"Forget it!" Barry yelled. "I don't want to play anymore!"

"I was just trying to win," Little Shaq said. "Let's start another game."

"It's no fun watching you play," Barry said. "You never let me shoot!"

Barry threw his controller down hard. It bounced off a toy truck and smashed right into the game console.

Barry looked up at Little Shaq, his eyes wide.

Little Shaq pulled the
game out of the machine.
"Look what you did!"
Little Shaq

yelled. "You broke it!"

"Who broke

what?" Little Shaq's

dad said, coming into

the room.

Barry and Little

Shaq both started to

talk at once.

"Rosa, can *you* tell me what happened?" Dad asked.

"Sure," she said. "Barry maybe accidentally broke the video game—"

"See!" Little Shaq shouted.

"But . . . ," Rosa went on. "It was kinda Little Shaq's fault too."

"Ha!" Barry said.

"Okay, okay," said Dad.

"Rosa, why don't you go fetch Malia and Tater for dinner."

Dad sat down between Little Shaq and Barry, and put his arms around their shoulders.

Little Shaq closed his eyes tight. He hated fighting.

Whenever he fought with his older sister, Malia, she always won, and fighting with his younger brother, Tater, was even worse.

But fighting with Barry was the worst of all.

Little Shaq breathed in Dad's woodsy scent and felt a little better.

"It was my favorite game," Little

Shaq said in a quiet voice. "Barry should have to buy me a new one."

"But it seems like you were both at fault, son," said Dad. "You don't think so?"

Little Shaq thought about the game at the rec center.

Suddenly, he remembered Barry calling for the ball on the court.

And he thought about the slam dunk from the video game.

Little Shaq's tummy sank for the second time that day.

Barry was right. Little Shaq never let him shoot.

Little Shaq turned to his cousin. "I'm sorry for hogging the ball," he said.

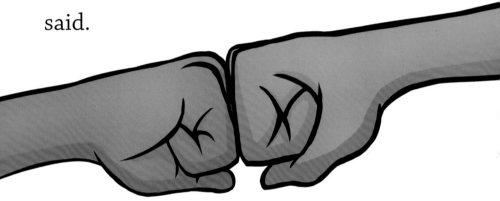

"It's okay," Barry replied. "I'm sorry for breaking the game."

Dad patted them both on the back.

"But what about the video game?"
Little Shaq asked. "It's still broken."

"Well," said Dad, "if you boys want

a new game, you'll have to work together to earn it."

Little Shaq looked over at Barry. He didn't know how they were going to do that.

Chapter 2
THE GAME PLAN

"All right, class," said Ms. Terpenny. "Settle down, please."

Little Shaq took a seat at his desk near Barry and Walter.

Rosa sat down next to Walter's twin sister, Aubrey.

Little Shaq yawned. He had stayed

up too late thinking about Barry and the broken video game.

Ms. Terpenny walked to the whiteboard.

"Can anyone tell me what we need to grow big and strong?" she asked.

Little Shaq raised his hand. "Ooh, I know!"

"Yes, Little Shaq?" said Ms. Terpenny.

"Food!" he said. "My mom says if I eat food that's good for me, I'll grow really tall."

"Your mom is right," said Ms. Terpenny. "And it looks like it's working!"

Little Shaq smiled.

"Food gives us energy," Ms. Terpenny went on. "And energy helps us grow. Do you know what else needs energy to grow?"

Rosa's hand shot up.

"Plants," said Rosa. "They get energy from the sun."

"A-plus, Rosa," said Ms. Terpenny.

"Plants also need air, soil, and water to grow," Ms. Terpenny continued.

She walked over to the science table.

"Each group has three pots of soil, two packets of seeds, and one watering can," she said. "We are going to plant our very own gardens."

"Cool!" said the Skipple twins.

Sometimes Walter and Aubrey thought exactly alike.

"Once a week we'll write down how tall the plants get," said Ms. Terpenny. "But you have to water them every morning or they won't grow at all."

"I'm really good at watering," said Barry. "I water Nana Ruth's plants every afternoon."

"I'm really good at watering too," said Little Shaq. "Mom has a garden out back."

All of a sudden, Little Shaq had an idea.

"Hey, Barry," said Little Shaq. "That's how we'll earn the money."

"What do you mean?" asked Barry.

"We are really good at watering," said Little Shaq. "I bet other people need their plants watered too."

"We'll start a business!" said Barry.

"Let's call ourselves . . . the O'Neal Green Team!" said Little Shaq.

Barry thought for a moment and smiled. "How about we work on the name together?"

"It's a deal!" said Little Shaq.

Later that afternoon Mom and Dad and Nana Ruth agreed to their plan.

Little Shaq and Barry were officially in business!

That Saturday, Barry and Little

Shaq loaded a red wagon with two watering cans.

The first house on their list belonged to Nana Ruth's friend Mr. Whitten.

There was a rose garden in Mr. Whitten's front yard.

"Hello there, boys!" Mr. Whitten called from his porch.

He was having tea with Nana Ruth.

"Hi, Mr. Whitten. Hi, Nana Ruth," said Little Shaq.

"Give those roses a good drink," Nana Ruth replied.

"And be careful of the thorns!" called Mr. Whitten.

Barry and Little Shaq took out the watering cans and sprinkled the soil with water.

It was so easy that Little Shaq guessed they would earn the money for a new game in no time.

Down the street, Mrs. Hobbs asked the boys to water the plants in her kitchen.

Some of her plants were hanging
high in the air.

Little Shaq reached
up to water them. They
were green and leafy.

He wondered
how Mrs.
Hobbs ever
watered them
without him.
Next door,
Ms. Emerson's

sunroom was lined wall-to-wall with plants of all shapes and sizes. It was like a jungle!

There were so many plants, Little Shaq was afraid he might knock them over.

Barry knew just what to do.

Taking tiny steps, he squeezed down the rows, sprinkling the plants as he went.

Barry even watered the prickly cactus all the way in the corner.

Little Shaq thought they made a
good team.

At the end of the block,

Mr. Rodriguez had a great big vegetable garden.

He grew all kinds of vegetables, like eggplant, corn, and zucchini.

But his tomatoes were famous!

Every summer he mixed them into a spicy salsa that he served at the neighborhood block party.

It tasted so good, there was always a line to get some.

Barry pushed the red wagon into Mr. Rodriguez's backyard.

He was careful to steer it clear of a few muddy patches, so the wheels wouldn't get stuck.

Little Shaq lifted the blue watering can. "Mine is almost empty," he said.

"Mine too," Barry replied. "Look, there's a hose."

"Good idea," said Little Shaq. "If you turn on the water, I'll fill the cans."

Barry turned the round knob on the water tap.

Little Shaq waited, but nothing came out.

"Turn it again," said Little Shaq.

Barry turned the knob once more.

Suddenly a stream of water gushed out of the hose.

"Ack!" Little Shaq yelled. He was soaking wet.

The hose slipped out of his hands and snaked across the yard, spraying water everywhere.

"Shut it off, Barry!" he yelled. "Shut it off!"

Little Shaq ran after the hose, but the ground was now covered in even more mud.

His feet slipped, and his legs scissored back and forth.

The next thing he knew, he was toppling into the garden, knocking over plants left and right.

"Oh no!" Little Shaq yelled. "Mr. Rodriguez's tomatoes!"

Barry turned off the water and hurried over to help.

"Are you okay, Little Sha—!" Barry's feet slipped too.

He landed in a puddle of mud.

SPLAT!

Mr. Rodriguez came outside to see what all the noise was about.

Barry and Little Shaq were covered in mud from head to toe.

"I'm really sorry," Barry said. "It

was my fault. I turned the water on too strong."

"No," said Little Shaq. "It was my fault. I let go of the hose."

Mr. Rodriguez smiled. "It's all right, boys."

Mr. Rodriguez picked up the hose. "It looks like the nozzle was turned too high. It was my fault."

"But your garden . . . Your tomato plants," said Little Shaq. "They're ruined!"

"Well, let's see what we can do about that."

Once Little Shaq and Barry had cleaned up inside, they joined Mr. Rodriguez out in the garden.

He showed them how to dig a hole

and replant the tomatoes, packing
the soil tight.

When they had finished, the
garden was as good as new.

Mr. Rodriguez told them they had
a career ahead of them.

Little Shaq liked the sound of that. He could see it now: O'Neals' Gardening: Watering and Planting Experts!

Little Shaq and Barry packed up their things and said thank you to Mr. Rodriguez.

It was time to go home.

Chapter 3
LAYUPS AND TURNIPS

A few weeks later, Little Shaq and Barry changed into their jerseys at the rec center.

They had been working together on Barry's layup every Saturday afternoon once they had finished gardening.

Barry's shot was getting really
good.

"Okay, Barry, are you ready to

do what we practiced?" Little Shaq asked his cousin.

"I think so," Barry replied.

"Great!" said Little Shaq. "Let's show everyone your new moves."

Coach Mackins blew his whistle.

TWEET!

Little Shaq lined up at center court across from Walter.

Coach Mackins tossed the basketball into the air.

Walter and Little Shaq jumped.
Little Shaq reached his hand up
high and knocked the ball toward his
teammates.

Barry got to it first.

He dribbled the ball right, dodging a defenseman.

He dribbled the ball left, dodging another.

Barry moved toward the basket, taking three quick steps.

He leaped, shooting the ball.

The ball bounced off the backboard and swished through the net.

It was a perfect layup.

"I did it!" Barry shouted.

Little Shaq slapped his hand high-five.

"Way to go, Barry!" Rosa cheered from the stands.

Little Shaq knew it was going to be a great game.

Barry scored two more baskets.

He was the MVP of the day.

After the last whistle blew, Little Shaq and Barry headed outside to wait for Nana Ruth.

Rosa was waiting for them at the curb. "Great game, Barry! Great game, Little Shaq!" she said.

"Thanks!" Barry and Little Shaq said together.

"Are you excited to buy your new video game tonight?" Rosa asked.

Little Shaq and Barry had finally saved up enough to replace the broken game.

Dad was taking them to the store after dinner.

Barry pulled out the envelope of money.

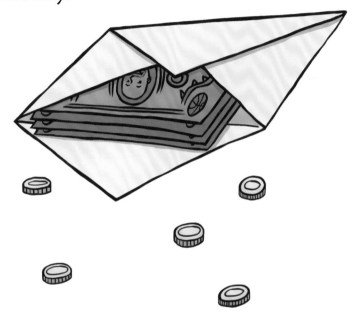

"We earned so much, we can even buy two games," Barry said.

Little Shaq turned and walked

along the curb, kicking at the dirt by the rec center's dried-up garden.

It looked so sad.

Then Little Shaq had an idea.

"Hey, Barry," he said, pointing to

the garden. "Do you think we're good enough to fix up this one?"

Barry thought for a moment. "It would need *a lot* of water, but, hey, we're experts!" he said. "And we have enough money to buy all the supplies."

The next weekend, Barry and Little Shaq loaded the red wagon with bags of soil and tools. They grabbed their watering cans and wheeled it all to the rec center.

Malia and Rosa were already in the garden pulling out the weeds.

Nana Ruth and Mr. Whitten arrived with pots of bright flowers for planting.

Mr. Rodriguez and Ms. Terpenny set up the vegetable patch.

Dad grilled burgers by the picnic tables. Mom helped Tater pour glasses of fresh lemonade and set out bowls of fruit, chips, and Mr. Rodriguez's famous spicy salsa.

It was a real garden party.

"Wow, this is looking great!" said Coach Mackins. "How can I help?"

"First, we need to add the new soil," said Little Shaq. "Maybe you can do that."

"Then we have to dig some holes," Barry went on.

"I wanna do that!" said Tater.

"Next we'll plant the seeds," said Little Shaq.

"That's my job," said Rosa. "We can plant tomatoes now and different vegetables each season."

"And pack them in tight," said Barry.

"I'm on it," said Malia.

"You boys sure know a lot about gardening," said Coach Mackins.

"There's one more step," said Little Shaq."

"We have to water everything," said Barry.

"But that's our job," said Little Shaq. "We are really good at watering." He turned to Barry. "Watering *and* layups."

Shaquille O'Neal is the author of the Little Shaq series, a retired basketball legend, a businessman, and an analyst on the Emmy award–winning show *Inside the NBA* on TNT. During his nineteen-year NBA career, O'Neal was a four-time NBA champion, a three-time Finals MVP, and a fifteen-time All-Star, and he was named the 1993 Rookie of the Year. Since his rookie year, he has been an ambassador for the Boys & Girls Clubs of America, a group with which his relationship goes back to his youth in New Jersey. Passionate about education, O'Neal earned his undergraduate degree from LSU, his MBA from University of Phoenix, and a PhD from Barry University.

www.shaq.com
@Shaq

Theodore Taylor III is the illustrator of the Little Shaq series and was awarded the Coretta Scott King/John Steptoe New Talent Award for his first picture book, *When the Beat Was Born*. An artist, a designer, and a photographer, Taylor received his BFA from Virginia Commonwealth University and lives in Washington, DC, with his wife and son.

www.theodore3.com